My Dog Never Says Please

by **Suzanne Williams**

pictures by **Tedd Arnold**

PUFFIN BOOKS

For Mark, my husband and sweetheart. –S.W.

To Sandy. And to Dean. Thanks! –T.A.

Weekly Reader is a registered trademark of the Weekly Reader Corporation
2005 Edition

PUFFIN BOOKS
Published by the Penguin Group
Penguin Putnam Books for Young Readers, 345 Hudson Street, New York, New York 10014, U.S.A.
Penguin Books Ltd, 27 Wrights Lane, London W8 5TZ, England
Penguin Books Australia Ltd, Ringwood, Victoria, Australia
Penguin Books Canada Ltd, 10 Alcorn Avenue, Toronto, Ontario, Canada M4V 3B2
Penguin Books (N.Z.) Ltd, 182-190 Wairau Road, Auckland 10, New Zealand

Penguin Books Ltd, Registered Offices: Harmondsworth, Middlesex, England

First published in the United States of America by Dial Books for Young Readers, a division of Penguin Books USA Inc., 1997
Published by Puffin Books, a division of Penguin Putnam Books for Young Readers, 2000

THE LIBRARY OF CONGRESS HAS CATALOGED THE DIAL EDITION AS FOLLOWS:
Williams, Suzanne.
My dog never says please/by Suzanne Williams; pictures by Tedd Arnold.—1st ed.
p. cm.
Summary: Tired of having to mind her manners, clean her room, and wear shoes,
Ginny Mae wishes she could trade places with the family dog.
ISBN 0-8037-1679-6 (tr: alk. paper).—ISBN 0-8037-1681-8 (lb: alk. paper)
(1. Behavior—Fiction. 2. Dogs—Fiction. 3. Family life—Fiction.) I. Arnold, Tedd, ill. II. Title.
PZ7.W66824My 1997 [E]—dc20 96-11950 CIP AC

Puffin Books ISBN 0-14-056725-9

Printed in the United States of America

The artwork was prepared with colored pencils and watercolor washes.

We'd just sat down to supper. I was hungry enough to eat
Snow White's poisoned apple. "Pass the potatoes!" I called out.

Ma raised an eyebrow. "Mind your manners, Ginny," she scolded. "That's no way to ask."

Then my pipsqueak brother Jack piped up. "I always remember to use the magic word," he said, like he had a little halo over his head.

Drat that Jack! Sometimes I wish I were a dog.

My dog never says "please," and no one thinks a thing about it. Easy life Ol' Red has got. Lying in the sun all day, barking at crows and cats, enjoying an occasional scratch.

I grabbed a chicken leg as the platter went sailing by and tore into it, pretending I was a dog with a bone.

"Chew with your mouth closed, Ginny girl," Pa said sternly. "No one wants to see what's going on inside your mouth."

"And use your napkin," added Ma. "You've got gravy on your chin."

"Ginny's disgusting," said Jack, making a show of cutting *his* chicken into teensy little bites.

I spit out a piece of gristle and swiped at my mouth. Wish they'd all just leave me alone. Ol' Red eats with his mouth open, and he never uses a napkin. They don't pick on him.

Why couldn't I be a dog?

There was some of Ma's sweet-tasting, mouth-watering cherry pie for dessert. Mine was gone in less time than it takes to tweak Jack's ear.

"Mmmm, mmmm," I said, running my tongue over my plate to get the last sticky drops of cherry juice. "You sure make the best pie in the world, Ma. How about a second helping?"

"Ginny Mae Perkins," said Ma. "You're hopeless. It's not good manners to lick your plate, and one helping of pie ought to be enough for a girl your size."

"But I'm growing," I said, wondering why she hadn't noticed *that*. Seems like she only looks at me to see my manners.

Anyway, what's wrong with licking your plate? It's a sign of respect. Shows how much you like something. My dog licks plates, and everyone pats him and tells him he's a good boy. Lucky Ol' Red.

I excused myself and hightailed it out of there, fixing to grab my jump rope and go outside.

But Ma had other ideas. She poked her head inside my room. "Seeing how you're done with supper," she said, "you can get started on this room of yours. Looks like a tornado went through here."

"Aw, Ma," I said. "I like it this way. Everything's right where I can see it, instead of hiding away in drawers."

Ma just gave me one of her looks, the kind that would burn a hole through an iron safe.

While I was picking things up, Ol' Red helped himself to my bed. He scrunched up in the covers, and settled down for a snooze. I scowled. "Why don't you get out in the yard and clean up your doghouse?" I told him.

But he just stretched and rolled over so I could scratch his belly. What a life he's got!

I finished my room, grabbed my jump rope, and headed for the back door, figuring to sneak out quietly before Ma could see me and think up something else for me to do. I had one foot out the screen door, when Jack, that little tattler, started hollering.

"Ma!" he bawled. "Ginny's going outside in her bare feet."

"Ginny Mae," Ma called, "put something on your feet. Pa's been hammering out back and there's likely to be nails around. First thing, you'll go poking one through your foot."

"Shoot, Ma," I said, "shoes crowd my toes." Truth is, I didn't know where my shoes were, now that my room was all cleaned up.

"Don't argue with your ma," Pa said. "Go put your shoes on."

I let go of the screen door. Ol' Red must've heard it squeal, 'cause all of a sudden he streaked by. Almost knocked me over as he pushed it open and leaped outside. I sure didn't notice any shoes on *his* feet. Talk about unfair! Seems to me a dog's life is much better than mine.

And the more I thought about it the madder I got, till finally I just sort of boiled over.

"You treat Ol' Red better than you treat me!" I yelled. "Correcting my manners, and making me work all the time. And I hate wearing shoes. I WANT TO BE A DOG!"

Then, try as I might to hold them back, tears poured out of my eyes like a darn waterfall. Ma hurried over and laid her hand on my shoulder. Jack snickered, but Pa shut him up with a look.

Pa scratched his head. "You want to be a dog?"

"Yup," I said, still sniffling. "I sure do."

Then, try as I might to hold them back, tears poured out of my eyes like a darn waterfall. Ma hurried over and laid her hand on my shoulder. Jack snickered, but Pa shut him up with a look.

Pa scratched his head. "You want to be a dog?"

"Yup," I said, still sniffling. "I sure do."

And the more I thought about it the madder I got, till finally I just sort of boiled over.

"You treat Ol' Red better than you treat me!" I yelled. "Correcting my manners, and making me work all the time. And I hate wearing shoes. I WANT TO BE A DOG!"

I let go of the screen door. Ol' Red must've heard it squeal, 'cause all of a sudden he streaked by. Almost knocked me over as he pushed it open and leaped outside. I sure didn't notice any shoes on *his* feet. Talk about unfair! Seems to me a dog's life is much better than mine.

And that's how I, Ginny Mae Perkins, ended up sleeping in a doghouse and begging for scraps. Ol' Red's real good about sharing though. I think he's even given me some of his fleas.

But I do miss Ma's cooking. Right now I hear pork chops sizzling through the open window. Ma must be getting supper ready. Sure does smell good. Maybe she'll save me a bone with a little meat on it.

There's lots of black clouds coming our way. Looks like it might rain.
Hmmm . . . I wonder if this doghouse leaks.

Pa says I can go back to being myself anytime I've a mind to.
So maybe I'll just saunter on in and wash up for supper.

But if that brother of mine dares to say even one teensy little word, why, I might just haul off and bite him on the leg.